P9-DIJ-600

 Published in the United States
by Puppy Dogs & Ice Cream, Inc.
ISBN: 978-1-949474-85-5
Edition: April 2020

For all inquiries, please contact us at:
info@puppysmiles.org

To see more of our books, visit us at:
www.PuppyDogsAndIceCream.com

This book is given with love

____

____

A friend is someone who hugs you,
When you're sad or feeling blue.
When things don't go as well as planned,
Your friend will comfort you and understand.

HAPPY BIRTHDAY

If you feel like stopping before you even start,

A friend encourages you so you don't lose heart.

Your friend will be there, waiting by your side,

To give you the strength you need inside.

If you have a special secret to share,

It's good to tell it to someone who will care.

When you don't want anyone to spread your news,

A true friend won't spill out any tiny hints or clues.

Gr.
4

You and your friend hang around together.

You share sunny jokes even when it's stormy weather.

Your friend always knows the things that make you smile,

Even if you don't always share the same style.

When you're passing time with your friend,
You wish the day would never end.
Sometimes the simplest things you do
Will stick in your memory like happy glue.

glue

Your best friend can teach you how to soar,

And, if you're shy, your friend might get you to roar!

Thanks to what your friend suggests, you might get to do

Something that makes you feel like a completely new you.

If you're anxious and feeling a bit scared,
Your friend can help you get prepared.
Soon you'll be brave enough to begin,
And your friend will cheer the loudest when you win.

Your friend can give you courage to face the unknown.
With your friend by your side, you know you're not alone.
Even if you're both scared, that's okay too.
You can help each other figure out what to do.

There isn't anything more wonderful than playing pretend.

You can make up stories and act them out with your friend.

You'll take turns playing the hero and the villain too,

Adventure awaits! There's treasure to pursue!

When you're discouraged, your friend can make you smile.

Silly jokes and antics lift you up after a while.

And when your friend is feeling down, you can be the one

To tell jokes, act silly, and change the mood to fun.

You might feel that you'll never have a friend,

But there's one easy way to make this feeling end...

Just reach out to someone who feels the same way as you,

It's the best way to start a friendship with someone new.

Your big sister can be an angel in disguise.

She watches over you so you don't do something unwise.

Even though she might be older, she's your friend too.

She's a special kind of friend who also loves you.

Sometimes you're so filled up, you want to explode.
Your brother will listen and let you unload.
Then, instead of telling you what he thinks you should do,
He guides you to the answer that is right for you.

TEST

As you grow up,

you'll attend lots of different schools.

And, when you get there,

you'll need to learn new rules.

Your teachers can be good friends...

they care about you too.

They want to see you be your best

in everything you do!

1 2 3
4 6 7

A friend isn't always a person,

pets are different than the rest.

Even though they cannot talk,

there are times when they know best.

They stay close by and cuddle you

when you're feeling sad

And bounce about and wag their tails

when you're feeling glad!

Your mom has always loved you

from the very first day.

She has a friendly way of teaching you

while you're both at play.

She shows you all the yummy foods

that home chefs can make,

And she'll be bursting with pride

when you bake your very first cake!

Sometimes your dad

is your best friend on Earth.

He encourages you to try harder

and understand your worth.

He'll help you step-by-step

to reach your every goal,

As you practice to get

the golf ball in the hole.

Your grandma is part of your family,
but she can also be your friend.
You know you can tell her anything—
on her advice you can depend.
She tells you many stories
about when she was your age,
And reads you books at bedtime
as you turn each page.

Going for a nature walk with your grandpa
is a very fun thing to do.
He knows about the plants and animals
and he'll be glad to teach you.
You can share your dreams with him...
and he'll say he understands.
As your friend, he loves to hear about
all your adventurous plans!

If you look in the mirror,

you'll see a friendly face looking back.

Be kind to yourself, be positive,

and you will stay on track.

Life sometimes gets bumpy,

but no matter who you are,

If you learn to be your own best friend,

you'll always be a star!

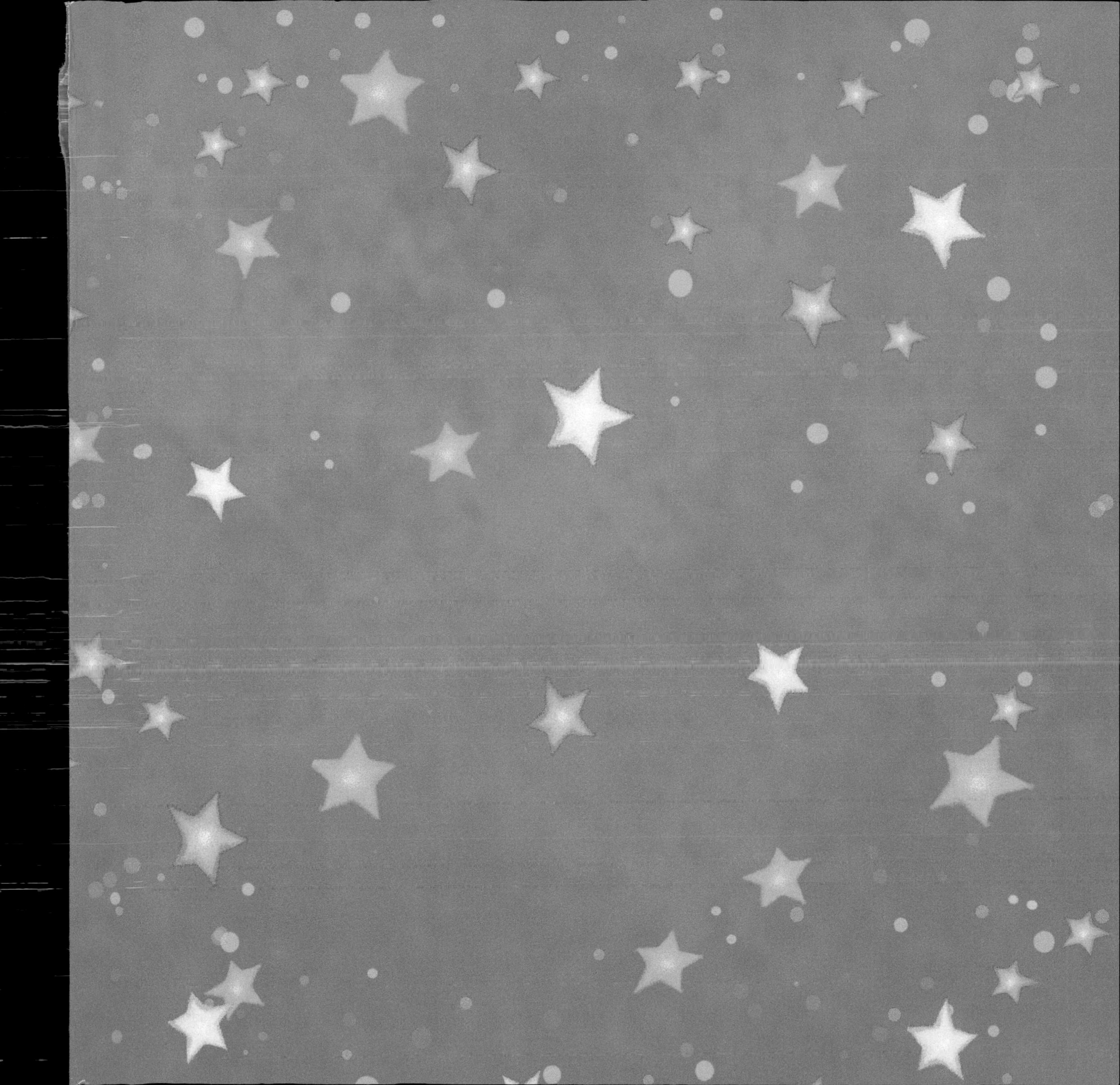

CPSIA information can be obtained
at www.ICGtesting.com
Printed in the USA
BVHW092225080421
604503BV00001B/30

9 781949 474855